WHo HOpS?

P9-DCV-580

Voyager Books
Harcourt, Inc.

Orlando
Austin
New York
San Diego
London

By
KATIE DAVIS

To my husband, Jerry,
who has helped me make my dreams come true
(kenahora ptew, ptew)

Copyright © 1998 by Katie Davis

All rights reserved. No part of this publication may be reproduced or
transmitted in any form or by any means, electronic or mechanical,
including photocopy, recording, or any information storage and retrieval
system, without permission in writing from the publisher.

For information about permission to reproduce selections from this
book, please write Permissions, Houghton Mifflin Harcourt
Publishing Company 215 Park Avenue South NY NY 10003.

www.hmhbooks.com

First Voyager Books edition 2001
Voyager Books is a trademark of Harcourt, Inc.,
registered in the United States of America and/or other jurisdictions.

The Library of Congress has cataloged the hardcover as follows:
Davis, Katie I.
Who hops?/Katie Davis.
p.   cm.
Summary: Lists creatures that hop, fly, slither, swim, and crawl,
as well as some others that don't.
[1. Animal locomotion—Fiction.   2. Animals—Fiction.]   I. Title.
PZ7.D2944Wh   1998
[E]—dc21   97-37175
ISBN 978-0-15-201839-9
ISBN 978-0-15-216412-6

SCP 15 14 13
4500400900

Who

hops?

Frogs hop.

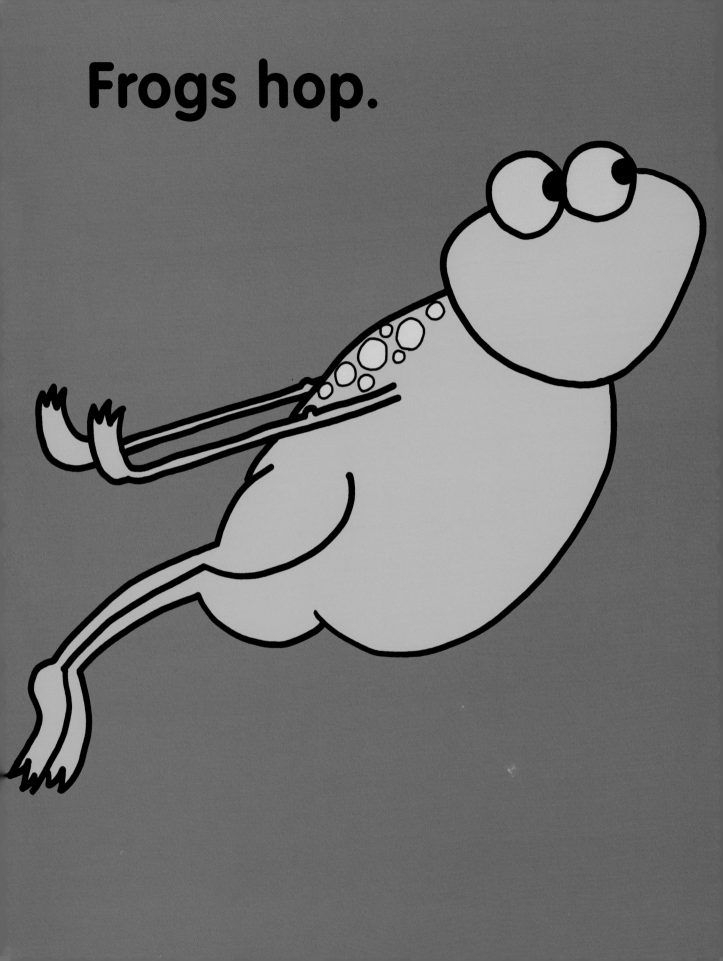

Rabbits
hop.

Kangaroos
hop.

Cows hop.

NO THEY DON'T!

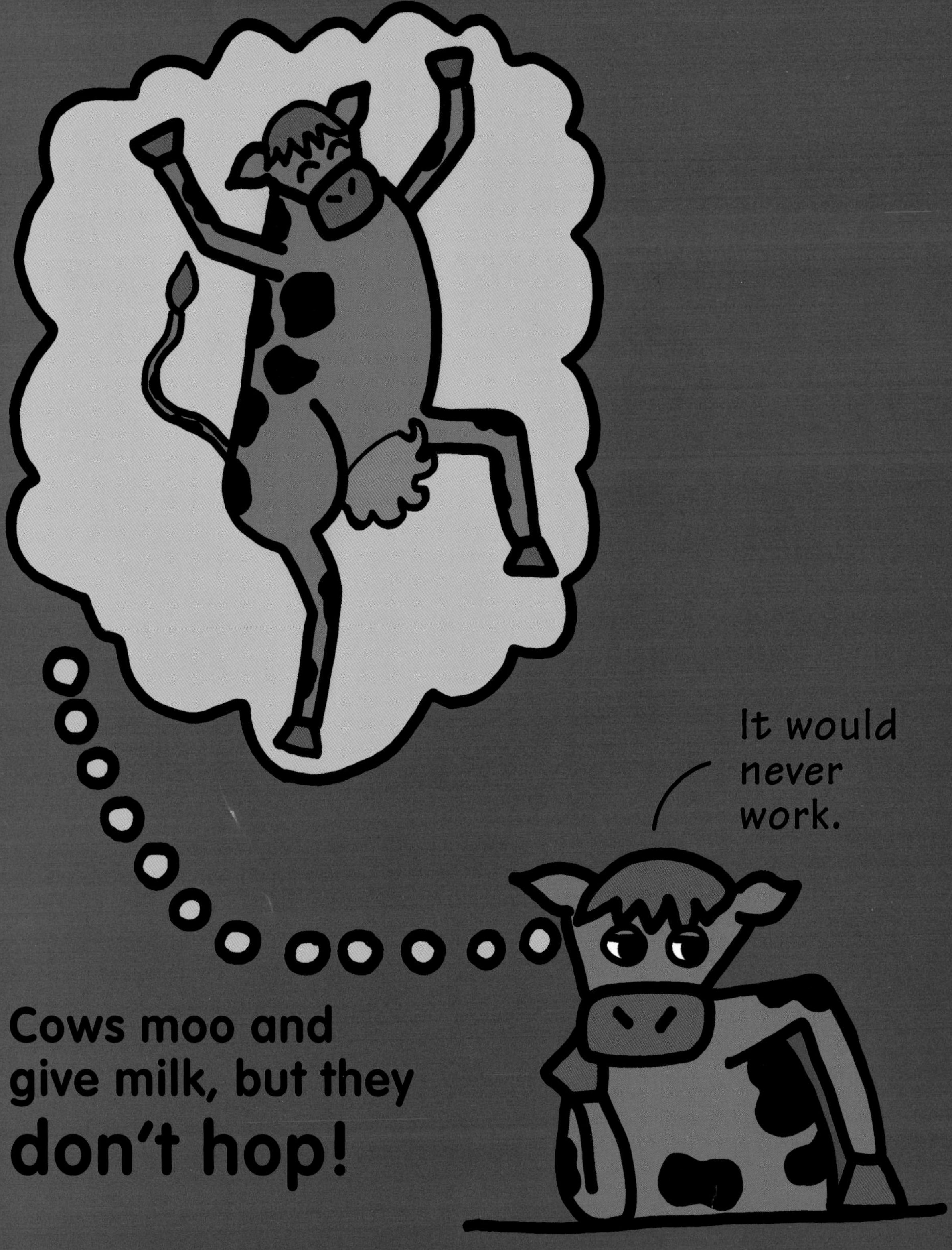

Cows moo and give milk, but they

don't hop!

Birds fly.

Bats fly.

Flies fly.

Rhinos fly.

Salamanders slither.

Snakes slither.

Snails slither.

Elephants slither.

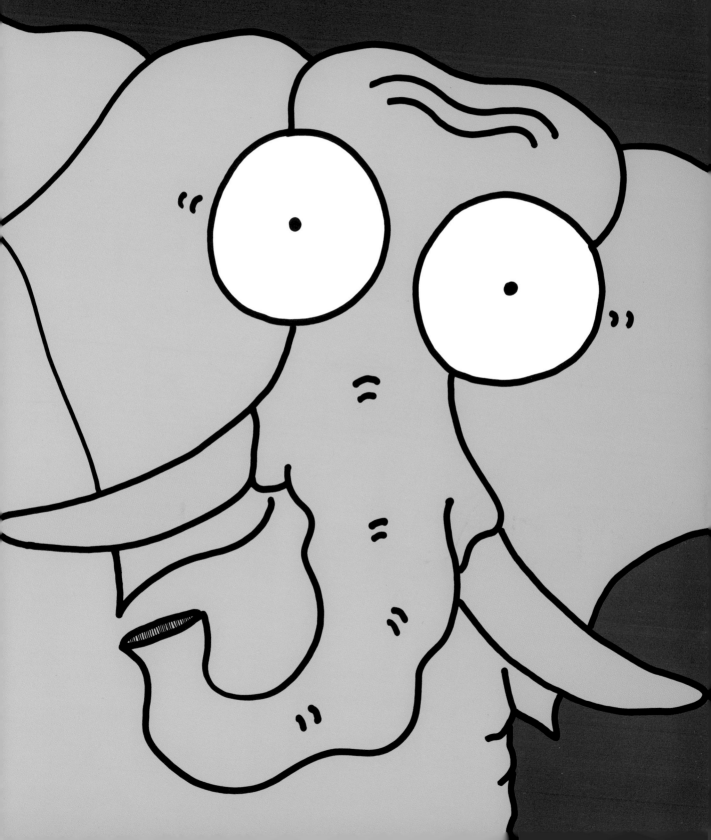

NO THEY DON'T!

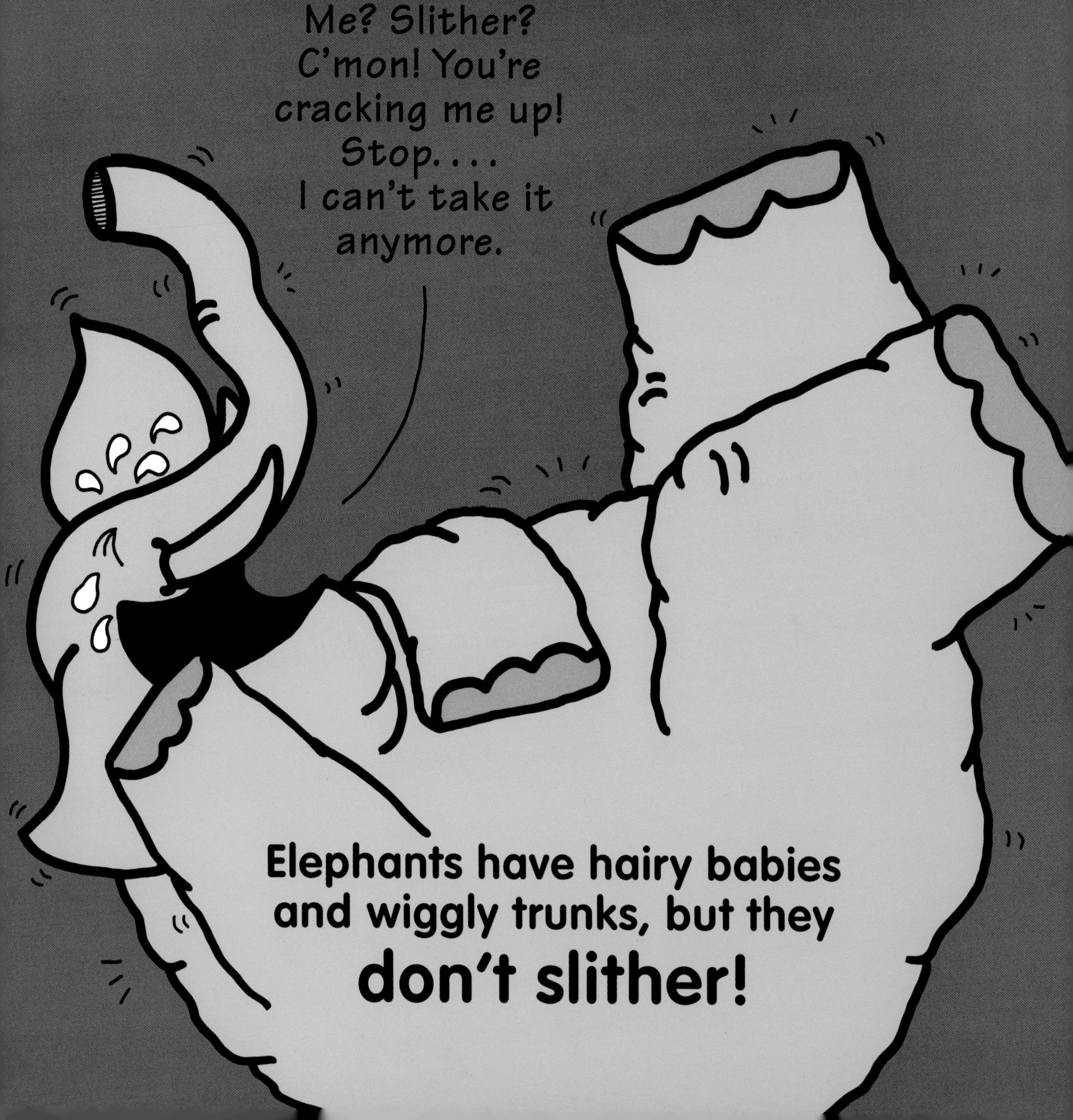

Elephants have hairy babies and wiggly trunks, but they **don't slither!**

Goldfish swim.

Sharks swim.

Whales swim.

Anteaters swim.

NO THEY DON'T!

Anteaters eat ants and have long sticky tongues, but they **don't swim!**

I just ate, so I really shouldn't go swimming anyway.

Spiders crawl.

Crabs crawl.

Crocodiles crawl.

Giraffes
crawl.

NO THEY DON'T!

Giraffes eat leaves and have really tall babies, but they **don't crawl!**

Who hops and flies and slithers and swims and crawls?

You do!

I give enormous and heartfelt thanks
to my own personal superhero triumvirate:
Peggy Rathmann, my mentor and friend, who hooked me up with
Steven Malk, my genius agent, who got me to
Susan Schneider, my editor, who brought this book
to a whole other level.

Without the support and constant hounding
from my amazing critique group—
Rosi Dagit, Molly Ireland, Maria Johnson,
Ainslie Pryor, Pam Smallcomb, and Ann Stalcup—
this book would have been all wrong.

And if Benny and Ruby,
my spirited and sweet children,
hadn't played Who Hops? with me in the first place . . .
Well, you get the picture.

The illustrations in this book were done in pen-and-ink with pre-separated colors.
The display type and text type were set in Vag Rounded.
Color separations by United Graphic Pte. Ltd., Singapore
Printed in China
Production supervision by Sandra Grebenar and Wendi Taylor
Designed by Linda Lockowitz